469.9841

W9-BSW-131

What if Everything Had Legs?

Scott Menchin

CANDLEWICK PRESS

NO STOPPING
ANYTIME

Mom, I'm sooooooo tired.

We're almost home, honey.
You can do it.

I can't — my legs hurt.

I made cupcakes this morning.
The faster we walk home,
the sooner you get one.

Mom, why can't the house have legs and walk to us?

Because then cupcakes could have legs and run away!

What if everything had legs?

If everything had legs . . .

then apples could land on their feet.

Worms would wiggle their toes.

A rake could jump in leaves . . .

and leaves would leave!

Cars could stroll, and snails could stride.

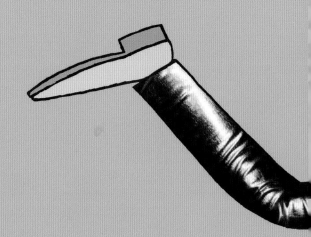

Rocks wouldn't roll.

But rolls could rock!

Mom, your laptop would become a legtop.

And toys would put themselves away!

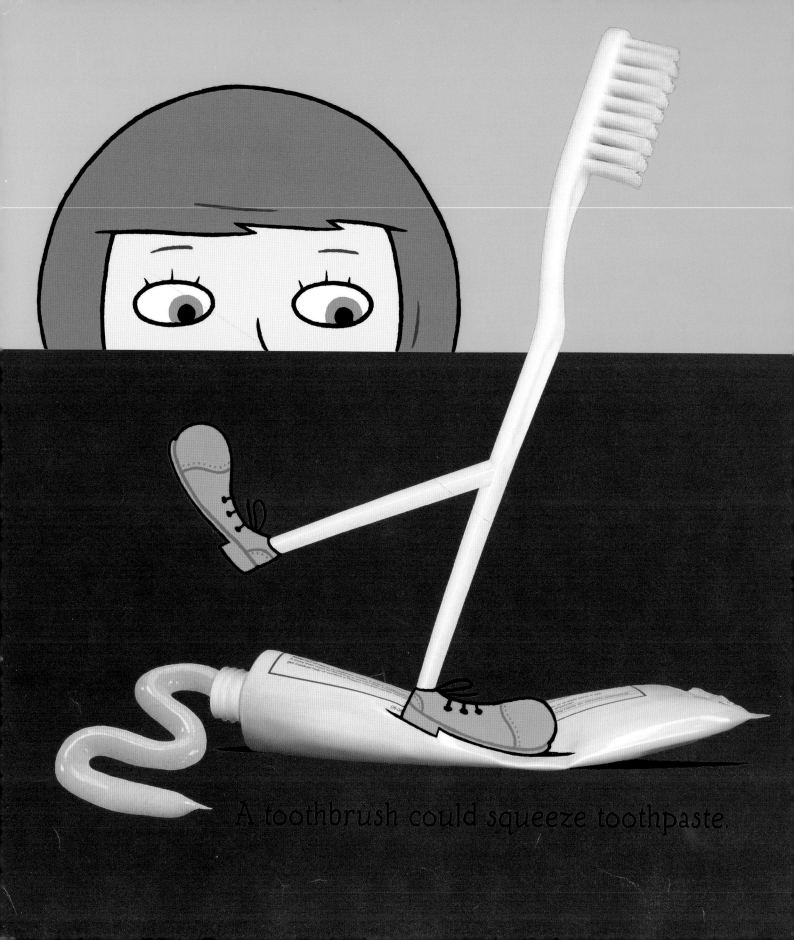

A toothbrush could squeeze toothpaste.

And bubbles would boogie-woogie.

Guess what, Mom? I'm not tired anymore!

And look, honey — we're home!

Mom?

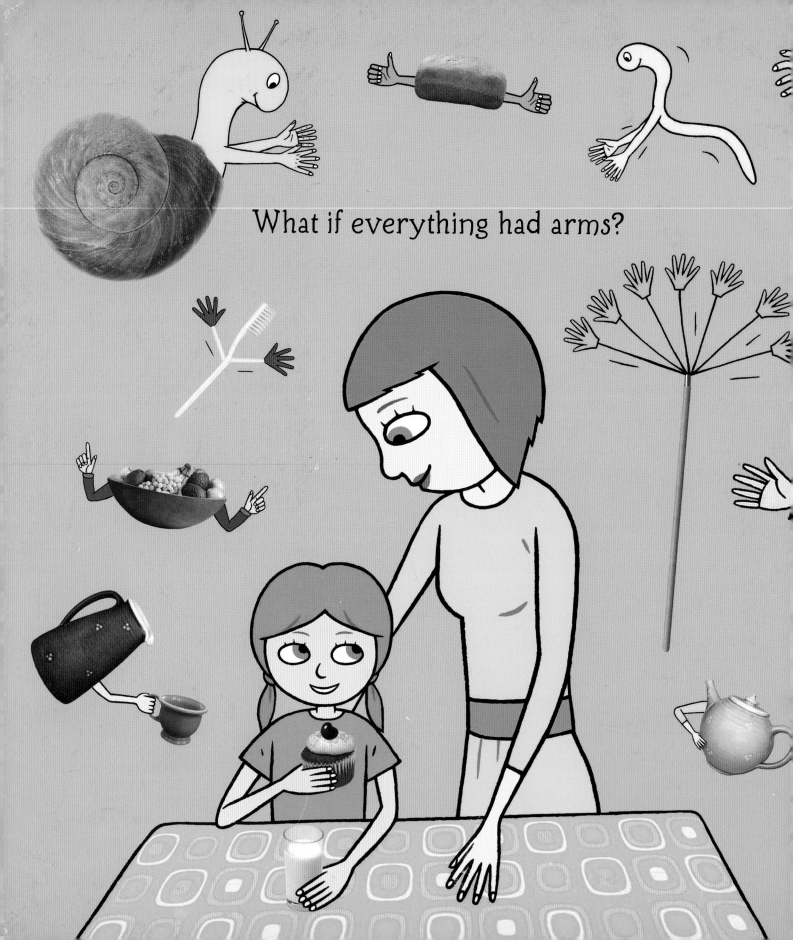

What if everything had arms?

To Karen Lotz

Copyright © 2011 by Scott Menchin

First edition 2011

Library of Congress Cataloging-in-Publication Data is available.

Library of Congress Catalog Card Number 2010038719

ISBN 978-0-7636-4220-4

11 12 13 14 15 16 LEO 10 9 8 7 6 5 4 3 2 1

Printed in Heshan, Guangdong, China

This book was typeset in Alghera.
The illustrations were drawn with pen and ink and colored digitally.

Candlewick Press
99 Dover Street
Somerville, Massachusetts 02144

visit us at www.candlewick.com